6/11

Lexile: _____290 L_____

AR/BL: _____2.0_____

AR Points: _____0.5_____

CORK & FUZZ

The Swimming Lesson

A Viking Easy-to-Read

by Dori Chaconas

illustrated by Lisa McCue

VIKING

AN IMPRINT OF PENGUIN GROUP (USA) INC.

VIKING
Published by Penguin Group
Penguin Young Readers Group, 345 Hudson Street, New York, New York 10014, U.S.A.
Penguin Group (Canada), 90 Eglinton Avenue East, Suite 700, Toronto, Ontario, Canada M4P 2Y3
(a division of Pearson Penguin Canada Inc.)
Penguin Books Ltd, 80 Strand, London WC2R 0RL, England
Penguin Ireland, 25 St Stephen's Green, Dublin 2, Ireland (a division of Penguin Books Ltd)
Penguin Group (Australia), 250 Camberwell Road, Camberwell, Victoria 3124, Australia
(a division of Pearson Australia Group Pty Ltd)
Penguin Books India Pvt Ltd, 11 Community Centre, Panchsheel Park, New Delhi – 110 017, India
Penguin Group (NZ), 67 Apollo Drive, Rosedale, North Shore 0632, New Zealand
(a division of Pearson New Zealand Ltd)
Penguin Books (South Africa) (Pty) Ltd, 24 Sturdee Avenue, Rosebank, Johannesburg 2196,
South Africa

Penguin Books Ltd, Registered Offices: 80 Strand, London WC2R 0RL, England

First published in 2011 by Viking, a division of Penguin Young Readers Group

1   3   5   7   9   10   8   6   4   2

Text copyright © Dori Chaconas, 2011
Illustrations copyright © Lisa McCue, 2011
All rights reserved

LIBRARY OF CONGRESS CATALOGING-IN-PUBLICATION DATA
Chaconas, Dori, date–
Cork and Fuzz : swimming lessons / by Dori Chaconas ; illustrated by
Lisa McCue.
p. cm.
ISBN 978-0-670-01281-7 (hardcover)
[1. Swimming—Fiction. 2. Opossums—Fiction. 3. Muskrat—Fiction.
4. Best friends—Fiction. 5. Friendship—Fiction.] I. McCue, Lisa, ill.
II. Title. III. Title: Swimming lessons.
PZ7.C342Cors 2011
[E]—dc22
2010033297

Viking ® and Easy-to-Read ® are registered trademarks of Penguin Group (USA) Inc.

Manufactured in China   Set in Bookman

For Nick

—D.C.

To Cameron, who loves to swim!

—L.M.

Chapter One

Cork was a short muskrat.

His house was in the middle of a pond.

He made it with sticks and reeds and
mud.

It was a muskrat kind of thing.

Fuzz was a tall possum.

His house was a hole in a tree.

He stuffed it with leaves and grass.

It was a possum kind of thing.

One wet muskrat and one dry possum. They were different, but they played together every day. It was a fun kind of thing.

One morning Fuzz went to look for Cork. Cork was in the middle of the pond. He was on top of his house.

"Cork!" Fuzz called across the pond.

"Will you come to my house to play?"

"Come over here!" Cork yelled back.

"Come to my house today."

Fuzz looked at the water.

"No!" he yelled. "I want you to come to

my house."

Cork swam across the pond.

He shook the water off his ears.

"You never come to my house," he said.

"We always go to your house. It is not fair."

Fuzz looked at the water again.

"I cannot go to your house," he said.

"I do not know how to swim."

Cork said, "Hmmmm . . ."

"Hmmmm what?" Fuzz asked.

"I know what we can do," Cork said.

"It will be something fun."

"Oh, good!" Fuzz said.

"I will teach you to swim," Cork said.

"Oh, bad!" Fuzz said.

Chapter Two

"Swimming is fun," Cork said.

"I do not want to get my feet wet,"
Fuzz said.

"You walk in puddles," Cork said.

"You get your feet wet all the time."

"I do not want to get my eyes wet,"
Fuzz said.

"Are you afraid?" Cork asked.

"I am not afraid," Fuzz said. "I do not
want to get my teeth wet."

"You are afraid!" Cork said.

Fuzz looked down at the ground.

"Okay, I am afraid," he said. "Being afraid is not fun."

Cork patted Fuzz on the back.

"Do not be afraid," he said. "I will teach you how to swim."

Cork found a grassy spot on the bank.

"Lie down here," he said. "On your belly."

Fuzz lay down. The grass tickled his chin.

He laughed.

"See," Cork said. "You are having fun already."

"I am having fun because I have a tickle!" Fuzz said. "I will not have fun when I am wet. I will not have fun when I am sinking."

"Just watch me," Cork said. He lay down
next to Fuzz. "Move your legs like this."
Cork paddled his front legs around and
around. He kicked his back legs up and
down.

Fuzz paddled his front legs. He kicked his
back legs.

"Look!" Fuzz yelled. "I am swimming!"

"Well, almost," Cork said. "You have to get
in the water first."

"Oh, bad," Fuzz said. He rolled onto his
back. He closed his eyes. He did not move.

Chapter Three

Cork poked Fuzz.

"Are you playing possum?" Cork asked.

"No," Fuzz answered. "I am floating."

"Oh, brother!" Cork said. "You are not floating! You are not even in the water yet!"

"Then I am thinking," Fuzz said.

"What are you thinking?" Cork asked.

"I am thinking that swimming is a muskrat thing to do," Fuzz said.

"Swimming is not a possum thing to do."

Fuzz opened his eyes. "Climbing trees is a possum thing to do. I think we need to forget swimming. I think we need to climb a tree instead."

"I am a muskrat," Cork said. "Muskrats cannot climb trees." Then he sighed.

"I cannot do a possum thing," Cork said. "And you cannot do a muskrat thing."

Cork sighed again.

"And you will never come to my house," he said.

Fuzz jumped up.

"Cork!" he said. "I know what to do!"

Fuzz pointed up at the tree.

"I can climb this tree," he said. "I can crawl
out on that big branch. When I get to the
end, I will jump down. I will jump down
right on top of your house!"

Cork shook his head and said, "Hmmm . . ."

"Hmmm what?" Fuzz asked.

"I think swimming would be safer,"
Cork said.

"But swimming is wet," Fuzz said.

"Climbing a tree is dry."

Fuzz climbed the tree. He crawled along
the big branch.

"I cannot watch!" Cork said. He covered
his eyes.

Chapter Four

"Hmmm . . ." Fuzz said.

"Hmmm what?" Cork asked. He peeked over his paws.

"This branch is not long enough," Fuzz said. "I am not over your house. I am still over the water."

"What are you going to do?" Cork asked.

"I am going to climb back down,"

Fuzz said.

Fuzz started to turn around. A bird

landed next to him on the branch.

The bird flapped in surprise to see

the possum. The possum flapped in

surprise to see the bird. Then Fuzz

fell out of the tree.

"YEOOOOOW!"

Cork had never heard such a loud
yell. Cork had never seen such a big
splash. And he had never felt such a
hard thump in his heart.

"Fuzz!" Cork yelled. He jumped into the
pond. He swam as fast as he could.

"Fuzz!" Cork yelled again. "Paddle!"

Fuzz paddled.

"Kick!" Cork yelled.

Fuzz kicked.

Paddle! Kick! Paddle! Kick!

And Fuzz began to swim. He swam and he
swam and he swam.

Fuzz swam all the way to Cork's house.

The two friends climbed out of the water
together.

"I swam!" Fuzz said. "I am a swimmer now!"

Cork put his arm around his friend's

shoulders. "I am so proud of you!" he said.

"I like your house," Fuzz said. "Thank you

for teaching me to swim."

"You are welcome," Cork said.

Then Fuzz said, "Hmmm . . ."

"Hmmm what?" Cork asked.

"You have taught me a muskrat thing,"
Fuzz said. "Tomorrow I will teach you a
possum thing."

"Oh, good!" Cork said.

"Tomorrow I will teach you to climb that
tree!" Fuzz said. "Then we will jump off
the branch together!"

"Oh, bad!" Cork said. "We will talk about it."

31

And so they did. One wet muskrat and
one wet possum. They sat on top of
Cork's house and talked. It was a best
friend kind of thing.